Serena's Secret isn't an ordinary story and you don't read it like an ordinary book. Here's how it works.

In the beginning, you meet the characters and learn a little about them — who they are, where they live, what they do. After that, the story depends on you. When Serena and her friend James have a decision to make, you get to make it. Your choice will take you to a different part of the book, where you'll discover what happened as a result of your decision. As you read you'll continue to make choices until you come to the end. When you finish one story go back, make different choices. There are many stories in the same book. What happens to Serena and James is up to you. You make the story happen—*it's your choice.*

IT'S YOUR CHOICE
Nonfiction Series
by David R. Stronck

Alcohol: The Real Story
Tobacco: The Real Story
Marijuana: The Real Story

IT'S YOUR CHOICE
Fiction Series
By Christine DeVault and Bryan Strong

Serena's Secret (Alcohol)
Danny's Dilemma (Tobacco)
Christy's Chance (Marijuana)

IT'S YOUR CHOICE
Teacher's Guides
are also available.

Attention: Schools and Organizations

IT'S YOUR CHOICE books are available at quantity discounts with bulk purchase for education, business or promotional use. For information, please write or call:

Special Sales Department
Network Publications
A Division of ETR Associates
P.O. Box 1830
Santa Cruz, CA 95061-1830
(408) 429-9822

Serena's Secret

Christine DeVault/Bryan Strong

Illustrated by Robert Ransom

Network Publications
a division of ETR Associates
Santa Cruz, CA
1987

Library of Congress Cataloging-in-Publication Data

DeVault, Christine.
  Serena's secret.

  (It's your choice)
  Summary: The reader tries to help Serena
make decisions about drinking alcohol and
shares with her the consequences of each decision.

  1. Plot-your-own stories. 2. Alcoholism—
Juvenile fiction. [1. Alcoholism—Fiction.
2. Conduct of life—Fiction. 3. Plot-your-own
stories] I. Strong, Bryan. II. Ransom, Robert,
1962- , ill. III. Title. IV. Series.
PZ7.D496Se 1987   [Fic]   87-18541

ISBN 0-941816-32-X (pbk)

For more information contact:
Network Publications
P.O. Box 1830
Santa Cruz, CA 95061-1830
(408) 429-9822
ISBN 0-941816-32-X

Serena's Secret

"Serena Williams, Rosemont High School," boomed a voice
from the ceiling.

Serena closed her eyes, bowed her head, and concentrated on her breathing. There's nothing else, she told herself. Just me. Just my breath. Arms, legs, hands, feet. Body and mind. And the balance beam.

Within moments, the glaring spotlights, the steamy air of the gymnasium, and the confusion of sounds and movement from the bleachers no longer existed for her. She raised her head and opened her eyes.

The noisy crowd sensed her readiness. The spectators grew still, their attention focused on the slim, dark girl in the white leotard, her long curls pulled back tightly into a pony tail. "Serena Williams, Rosemont High School," boomed a voice from the ceiling. With quick, easy movements, she mounted the beam.

At fifteen, Serena was one of the youngest members of her high school's gymnastics team. She was already known for her grace and skill, especially on the balance beam. Her coach thought she was "Olympic material." He had urged her parents to let her train for tryouts.

They had firmly refused to even consider it. "Her schooling comes first. We want Serena to be able to attend a top-notch university."

Still, as he watched his daughter gracefully perform,

Donald Williams felt proud.

"She's perfection itself, isn't she, Donald?" whispered Serena's mother, Denise. They held each other tightly as they watched their only child, their greatest joy, in the pool of light below them.

From several rows above Serena's parents, two pairs of eyes were closely following her. "Nice moves, huh?" whispered Mark Ishida, digging his elbows into James Pryce's ribs. "How well you know her?"

"Shut up, man," James muttered. Not well enough, he thought. Not well enough.

But for Serena there was no audience, no other time or place. She knew her routine so well, it seemed as if her body was on automatic pilot. Turn, pose, dip, squat, roll forward.... This was the payoff for years of practice, for hours spent toning every muscle and learning all the movements her body was capable of. As long as there was no distraction....

There was no distraction. Serena dismounted from the beam with a breathtaking cartwheel, ending what she knew was a perfect routine. She didn't need to see the numbers the judges scratched on their score cards. She didn't need to hear the announcer's voice or the cheers from the crowd to know how she'd done. She could feel when it was right.

She walked lightly to her seat among her teammates and returned their smiles and hugs of congratulation.

But the noise and activity around her still did not seem quite real. For the rest of the meet she sat in a daze.

The final scores were totalled (Rosemont High, by two points). The team and a good portion of the audience were swarming around the gym, laughing, crying, and hugging.

Serena's good friend Tracy Carter, who was also on the team, was hopping up and down like a rabbit, holding onto Serena's arm. "You did it," she squealed. "Two points! *You* did it, Rena. You're so beautiful!"

"Everybody did their part, Trace. You did. Everyone did," Serena replied gently. Then she laughed, "Turn loose of my arm, girl. You're stopping the circulation."

A bundle of energy in a fluffy pink sweater rushed at Serena and threw its arms around her neck. "Ooh, you're so great! You're so totally amazing! I love you!"

Sometimes Serena was embarrassed by Christy's noisy enthusiasm, but tonight she allowed herself to join both her friends in their bouncing dance.

The three girls stood together, catching their breath. Serena noticed her parents standing a little way off. She watched them for a few moments as other parents came over and shook their hands, congratulating them on their daughter's performance. Her dad looked over and caught her eye. " 'Scuse me," Serena said, "My folks."

As she started toward her parents, she felt a hand on her shoulder. A warm hand, kind of heavy. She looked: a brown hand; a boy's hand. She turned and felt the heat rush to her cheeks. "Hello, James." She smiled up into a pair of liquid dark eyes. She couldn't believe she'd actually managed to speak.

"Hey, Serena, I just wanted to say you were great. Beautiful." James' voice was low and soothing, like water running over smooth rocks in a deep brook.

"Thanks," she heard herself saying. "But really I didn't do all that much. It's the whole team that...." Her voice trailed off. She realized his hand still rested on her shoulder. And people were looking at them. Especially the girls. At least half the girls at Rosemont were after James Pryce.

She knew him a little. He was a year ahead of her, but they were in the same geometry class. She'd let him copy her homework a couple of times during lunch, and he'd always smiled and promised to pay her back.

"Ahem." Beside her, her father pretended to clear his throat. He looked at James. James dropped his hand. "Baby," her dad said, bursting into a smile and pulling her to him in a smothering bear hug. "We're so proud of you."

"Yes," echoed her mother, joining them. "We're so proud."

Serena hugged her mother too, then glimpsed, from the corner of her eye, that James was still standing in the same spot. Tracy and Christy were still there too, staring at James with their mouths practically hanging open.

"So," said Serena's dad, taking charge of the situation as usual, "Who's this young man?"

"Oh, Daddy, this is...I was...uh..."

"James Pryce, sir." James stepped forward, offering his hand.

"Not Henry Pryce's son by any chance?" inquired her father.

"Yes sir," James replied. He shook her mother's hand. "Pleased to meet you, ma'am."

"I've done some business with your father. He's a good man," pronounced her dad.

Serena stared at her father. Here he was, making small talk with possibly the coolest guy in the entire school. And the possibly coolest guy in the entire school was answering as if it were the most normal thing in the world.

"Actually, sir, I was going to ask you if you would allow Serena to go to a small party with me tonight."

Serena took a deep breath, and then another one, while she waited for her dad's reply. She glared a warning at Tracy who was starting to squeal again.

"Well, I don't know," began her dad.

He's going to say no, I know he's going to say no, Serena thought. She tried to give him her most responsible, grown-up look.

"Let me discuss this with Mrs. Williams." He took his wife's arm and moved off a few steps.

James touched Serena's arm gently. "I'm sorry. I meant to ask you first if you wanted to go to the party at Randall Thomas' house. Some of the guys from my group are gonna be there. I don't know what kind of music you like, but...uh...we might jam a little and...uh...maybe you might enjoy it." He looked at her hopefully.

She smiled. "I'd love to. But I don't know if my folks will let me. I'll go see."

Serena walked quickly to where her parents stood, pausing only to cross her eyes and stick out her tongue at Tracy and Christy who were now striking silly poses behind James' back.

"Please, Daddy. It's really important to me. Please." She cast a pleading look at her mother.

"Donald," her mother said. "As long as we know where she is and she's home by 11:00, maybe it would be all right for her to go."

Serena's father looked down at her. He looked very serious. "Baby," he said, "here's how it is. Your mama and I were planning to take you to dinner at Philippe's. This is such a special occasion, we wanted to do something really nice for you."

He took her aside a few steps. "This is very important to your mother. I think you should come with us."

Serena looked over at her mother, who smiled and came and put her arm around her daughter. "You can choose, baby. Can't she, Donald?"

"I suppose so, Denise," replied Serena's father. "She's old enough to make intelligent decisions." He looked straight into Serena's eyes as he spoke.

Oh, help! Serena thought. I *really* want to be with James. But I don't want to disappoint my folks. What should I do?

What did Serena do?

Choice A
If you think Serena chose to go to dinner with her parents,
turn to page 8.

Choice B
If you think Serena chose to go to the party with James,
turn to page 15.

Serena sighed. She walked back to where James stood. "I'm sorry," she said. "My folks are expecting me to go out with them, and I just can't let them down. Maybe some other time?" She put her hand lightly on his arm. Now that she had a chance to spend time with James, she hated the idea of being apart from him. I'm so stupid, she thought. Why did I say I couldn't go?

James covered her hand with his for a moment. "It's all right. I understand. I'll be calling you. Okay?"

"Okay. Bye." She tried to give him her brightest smile, but she felt the tears starting to form behind her eyes. She turned quickly and headed for the door.

Cheers from her teammates welcomed Serena to the locker room. The girls bounced and swirled about, hugging and congratulating each other again. Serena allowed a few tears to fall and then let herself be caught up in the activity.

"Okay, that's enough," she protested, prying Tracy's arms from around her neck. "My parents are waiting for me." She found her locker and leaned her forehead against the coolness of the metal door.

Tracy was right behind her, followed closely by Christy, who was ready to burst with curiosity. "So what was that all about? What did he say? What did *you* say? Are you gonna go out with him? Is your dad gonna let you?"

Serena held out her hand. "I'll never wash it again,"

she announced. "He touched this hand!" Then she sighed. "I hafta go to dinner with my folks. But he said he'd call," she added with more cheerfulness than she actually felt. She gathered her things and headed for the showers.

"Don't get your hand wet!" shouted Tracy.

* * *

An hour later, Serena and her parents were sitting in elegant Philippe's Restaurant. The candlelight, fresh flowers, and sparkling crystal glasses would ordinarily have delighted Serena. But tonight she was having trouble being cheerful.

Her mind kept going back to James' words: "I'll be calling you." He seemed so far away now. She wondered what he was doing, who he was with. Maybe he'd met someone else, fallen in love, and would never call. With her fork, she pushed a mushroom around her plate.

Serena's thoughts were interrupted by a tinkling sound. Her father was tapping his wine glass with the edge of his knife. "Ahem," he began. "I would like to propose a toast." He raised the glass. "To the finest daughter anyone could hope for. May you always succeed."

"Hear, hear!" her mother chimed in, clinking her glass against her husband's.

"To the finest daughter anyone could hope for," said Serena's father.

They really are good parents, Serena thought, hoping her smile was convincing. She raised her glass to them. "To my parents. You guys are great." Noticing she'd finished her sparkling grape juice, Serena asked if she could have a little wine for her toast.

"I don't think so, baby," her father said. "This is a public restaurant after all. We wouldn't want to get them in trouble, would we? If we were home, I'd have no objection to you having a bit of wine on a special occasion. But this is different."

Serena's mother took her glass from her and poured in a bit of water. Serena drank it obediently, but inside she was boiling.

It's just like them, she thought. Everything has to be so proper. A public restaurant! Who would know or care if I had a couple of sips of wine? Them and their rules. And they never have more than a glass of wine when they go out. They're so careful. They're always talking about the dangers of drinking and driving. They wouldn't dream of taking a risk. Sometimes I wonder if they have any fun at all.

"I think I'd like to go home now," she said.

"Don't you want dessert, sugar?" her mother asked. "Chocolate mousse? Cherry cheesecake?"

"Please, Mom. Can't we just go home?" Suddenly she was very tired.

* * *

Serena slept soundly that night. At 6:30, out of habit, she woke up. She looked at the clock, remembered it was Saturday, and went back to sleep.

When the phone rang she was dimly aware of it but didn't bother struggling out from under the covers to answer. Moments later her mother tapped at her door. "Are you awake, baby? Phone's for you."

She reached for the bedside extension. "Hello?"

"Hey, Sleeping Beauty! This is your prince!"

All at once, Serena was wide awake.

"Hi." She wondered if her smile could travel through the phone lines. "James? How are you? How was the party?"

"It was all right."

They talked for a while—about the party, about school, about music, about nothing in particular.

"So," James said. "You doing anything later on?"

"Uh, I don't know. When later on?"

"Well, I was gonna go over to the mall with Mark around noon. Just to hang out, you know. Maybe play some games at the arcade."

"My parents would never allow their 'baby' to hang out at the mall, but I'll think of something. I'll try to get over there."

"Okay. Later."

After she hung up, Serena hurriedly dialed Christy's number.

"He just called me! He wants me to meet him." She explained her predicament to her friend.

"Hang up," said Christy. "I'm gonna call and ask you to go shopping with me. I have to get new shoes for gym. Mine are falling apart and I need your advice on what kind to get. But I absolutely have to be home by 2:00 'cause we're going to my grandma's. Do you think that'll work out for you?"

"It sounds great, Christy. Thanks."

When Christy called back, Serena asked her mother if she could ride her bike to the mall to help her friend shop for gym shoes.

"My, but you're the popular one this morning," observed her mom. "Do you think you'll be back by 3:00?"

I need more time, Serena thought. James might want to spend the whole afternoon with me. But Mom and Dad'll kill me if they find out! Should I play it safe and come home early? Or should I try to get the whole day free? I could say I'm going over to Christy's after. Maybe I should take a risk for once....

What did Serena do?

Choice A
If you think Serena chose to tell her mother she'd be home right after shopping,
turn to page 31.

Choice B
If you think Serena chose to tell her mother she was going to Christy's and would be home later,
turn to page 35.

Serena took a deep breath. She put a hand on each parent's arm. "Mom. Dad. I'm sorry, but this is so important to me. Really, it is. I'll be home by 11:00, I promise."

"That's all right, sugar." Her mother patted her shoulder. "You go have a good time."

Donald Williams walked over to James. "Well, young man. You take care of our baby girl now. We expect her home at 11:00 sharp."

"Daddy, please," hissed Serena through clenched teeth. "I'll be fine." Sometimes her dad embarrassed her so much she wished she could disappear.

James didn't seem to mind though. "Yes sir, 11:00 it is." He shook her father's hand. "See you out front, Serena."

Serena kissed her folks hurriedly. "Thanks, Mom. Thanks, Dad. See you later." She ran for the door.

Cheers from her teammates and friends welcomed Serena to the locker room. The girls bounced and swirled about, hugging and congratulating each other again.

"Okay, that's enough," she laughed, prying Tracy's arms from her neck and heading for her locker. "I've gotta get ready. I need your help!"

"You mean you're actually going out with James Pryce?" Tracy asked in amazement.

"Where are you going?" Christy chimed in. "What

"Wow! Is this your car?" Serena asked James.

did your folks say? What did he say?"

"Yes, I'm really going out with him. We're going to a party at Randall's."

*   *   *

Fifteen minutes later, James saw Serena emerge from the gym. "You look great," he said. He hoped it would be okay at Randall's. Some of those parties could be pretty rowdy. They walked across the parking lot to a sleek silver sports car.

"Wow! Is this your car?" she asked.

"Actually, it's my dad's. This is just the second time he's let me use it. He says he'll have me for lunch if anything happens to it."

"You must be a good driver. I mean, if he trusts you with his new car."

"Yeah, I guess. I try. Some of my friends get on my case 'cause I won't drink with them if I'm driving. But I can handle that. It's harder to handle my old man when he's ticked off. He had some bad experiences mixing drinking and driving. So I figure he knows what he's talking about."

*   *   *

Randall Thomas was a senior at Rosemont High. He had a reputation for giving wild parties. Serena had heard that the police had broken up several. She hoped that wouldn't happen tonight. She wondered about Randall's parents. Where were they when this was going on? Maybe they just didn't care what Randall did. My parents would freak out if I had a party like this, she thought. She hoped she'd act okay. She didn't want James' friends to think she was uncool.

There were already quite a few people at the party. Most of them were standing in small groups in the darkened living room. Some were drinking cans of soda or beer. A few red and blue bulbs provided what light there was, casting weird shadows on the bare walls. The stereo blared loudly.

James introduced Serena to a few people. She also saw a few kids she already knew. She greeted Melissa Mendez and Shawna Rains whom she'd known slightly since sixth grade. Melissa and Shawna always seemed to know where the fun was. They greeted Serena warmly. She started to relax a little.

"Well, I guess I'll go help set up the equipment," said James. "You want a coke or something?"

Serena smiled and nodded. Hmm, she thought. He didn't even ask if I wanted a beer. I wonder if he thinks I'm too immature. Actually, Serena had tried beer before and had hated the taste. But, she thought, at least he could have asked!

"Looks like you're gettin' some class, James," teased Shawna when he returned with Serena's soda.

"That's right." James gave Serena's arm a brief squeeze and disappeared into the dining room where his band was setting up.

Serena turned to Melissa and Shawna. "Let's go out on the porch for some fresh air."

Outside, Serena set her can of soda on the porch railing. She breathed the cool night air and looked around. A guy was coming up the front steps.

It was Josh Keller. His parents were both attorneys in the same law firm as Serena's father. She'd known him for ages. In some ways he was like a big brother to her.

"Serena! What are you doing here? I didn't think this was your kind of scene!"

"What do you mean by that, Josh?" she asked icily. She leaned lightly on the railing, causing her soda to tumble into the bushes below. "Oh no, there goes my drink!"

Josh looked at her over the top of the bag he was carrying. "Who'd you come with, anyway?"

"James Pryce, if it's any of your business," Serena snapped.

"Hey, lighten up," Josh said. "James is a good man. I'm sorry about your drink. You want a wine cooler?

C'mon inside and I'll get you one."

Serena wondered what a wine cooler tasted like. Maybe it won't be as bad as beer, she thought. And I'd probably look more like I belonged here if I had wine instead of soda.

"I'm going inside too," said Melissa. "I can get you a coke or something if you don't want the wine cooler."

Serena smiled at her. That's nice of her, she thought. I guess it's not really necessary to drink alcohol....

What did Serena do?

Choice A
If you think Serena decided to accept the wine cooler,
turn to page 21.

Choice B
If you think Serena decided to accept a soda from Melissa instead,
turn to page 29.

"I'd love a wine cooler," Serena said with a smile, following Josh into the house.

Josh fished a bottle from his bag, twisted its top off and handed it to Serena. She took a couple of big gulps. Not too bad, she thought. Thank goodness. She drank some more.

"Thanks, Josh." She scanned the crowded room, looking for a familiar face.

"There you are!" James appeared suddenly at her side. He looked relieved. "I thought maybe you ran away."

"Never!" she replied, putting her arm through his. She was surprised at her own boldness. "I was just talking to Josh."

"Hey, Josh!" The guys punched each other a few times. Then James put his arm around Serena. "We're gonna start in a minute. I just wanted to make sure you're okay." He glanced at her wine cooler bottle but didn't say anything.

"I'm having a great time, James, really. Go on and play now. I'll be fine."

"Okay. You be good, hear?" He leaned over and kissed her cheek. "You're beautiful," he whispered.

Serena's knees felt weak. She gulped some more of her drink.

"There're a few girls here who'd give anything to be in your shoes," said Melissa, coming over to Serena.

"I know." Serena raised the bottle to her lips again and was surprised to find it empty.

"I'm gonna get another beer," Melissa said. "You want another one of those?"

Serena started to say yes, but then she stopped to think about it. She felt relaxed, warm, carefree. Was it possible she was already a little drunk? She'd heard you weren't supposed to drink on an empty stomach. She hadn't eaten anything since way before the gymnastics meet. How long ago that all seemed!

She thought about her team, her coach, and her long hours of training. She knew that drinking alcohol could be physically damaging. She'd always been very proud of her healthy, well-toned body. She didn't want to harm herself in any way. Then she thought about her parents. What if they found out?

On the other hand, she felt perfectly in control of herself. Maybe it's just love I'm feeling, she thought. She giggled.

"Well," Melissa demanded, "you want something or not?"

What did Serena do?

Choice A
If you think Serena accepted a second alcoholic drink,
turn to page 24.

Choice B
If you think Serena did not *accept a second alcoholic drink,*
turn to page 29.

"Sure, thanks." Serena smiled at Melissa. The band's first chords filled the air with a vibrant, pulsing sound.

Then Melissa was back, holding out a can to her. "No more coolers so I got you a beer." She flopped into the other chair and drank her own beer thirstily. "They sound pretty hot tonight, don't they?"

Serena nodded. She had accepted the can, but she hesitated before opening it. I hate beer, she thought. Why am I doing this? Then she popped it open and took several quick swallows. At least it's cold, she told herself.

Serena sighed. She had to admit she was nervous. First, there's James, she thought. I like him a lot and I'm afraid he might not like me. I really don't want him to think I'm a baby. Then, there're all these other people. Most of them are older than I am. They act nice, but who knows what they're thinking! The beer in her hand gave her a feeling of security, at least for the moment.

She drank some more. She glanced over the rim of the can, and her eyes met James'. He wasn't smiling. She was trying to figure out what his look meant when Randall asked her to dance.

"Okay." Her knees felt a bit wobbly and she grabbed his arm to get her balance.

* * *

As he played, James watched Serena.

He was worried. He'd promised Serena's folks he'd take care of her, but it looked like he wasn't doing a very good job.

She looks like she's enjoying herself, he thought. He watched as she quit dancing long enough to return to her can of beer and finish it off. Then she was out on the floor again, turning, shaking, laughing.

Serena stumbled and James felt his fingers seem to stick on the guitar neck. "Sorry," he mumbled as the bass player looked over at him.

James concentrated on his playing then. But when the number was finished he put down his guitar. "You guys keep on playing. I'll be back in a minute." He looked around for Serena.

Now you've really done it, he told himself. First you leave her on her own. Then you just stand there and watch her drink booze. And now you've gone and lost her! He pushed his way toward the front door.

He heard Serena's laugh and headed for the group of people standing at the far end of the porch.

Why am I so mad? he asked himself. Nothing terrible has happened. If she doesn't drink any more she'll probably be okay. But what if she keeps drinking? What should I say?

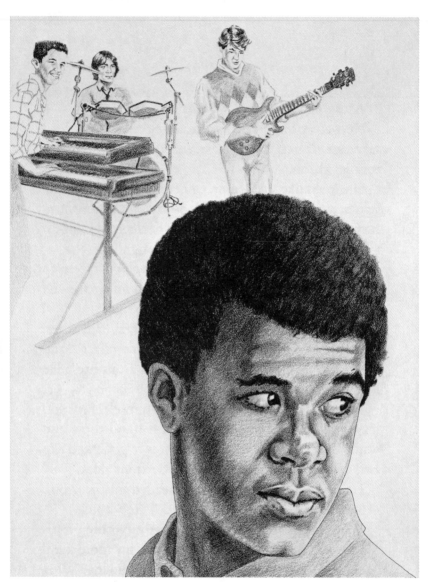

As he played, James watched Serena.

He didn't want Serena to drink any more. He didn't want her parents angry at him. But he didn't want Serena angry at him either.

If I try to tell her what to do, he thought, she might never go out with me again. But if she keeps drinking and her parents find out, they'll never let her go out with me again. Besides I really don't like being around people who've had too much to drink. I'd better be honest with her. So I'll just tell her right now and get it over with, he thought.

"Oh, hi, James. I'm so glad you're here," said Serena when she saw him. She gave him a little hug.

"Hi," he said. She seems fine, he thought. On second thought, maybe I don't need to say anything.

What did James do?

Choice A
If you think James told Serena he was bothered by her drinking,
turn to page 48.

Choice B
If you think James decided not *to say anything to Serena about her drinking,*
turn to page 50.

"Uh, I'll take a coke," Serena answered. "Thanks." Then the band's first chords burst out to fill the room with a vibrant, pulsing sound. She moved closer to the band.

Soon Melissa found her and held out a can to her. "Here's your coke. I got myself one, too. I like beer okay, but I get a horrible headache if I drink too much." She flopped into the other chair. "They sound pretty hot tonight, don't they?"

Serena agreed. She opened the soda and sipped at it. She glanced over the rim of the can and her eyes met James'. She smiled and raised the can a little in a toast. He nodded and a slight smile played around his lips.

Then Randall asked her to dance.

As she danced, she was aware that James was watching her. She was used to being watched, but somehow this was different, special.

Someone lurched into her then, throwing her off balance. Randall caught her arm to steady her. The girl who had fallen against her was sprawled on the floor.

"Shawna! Are you all right?" Serena bent to help her friend.

"'Scuse me, S'rena." Shawna got to her feet, swaying slightly. "Hey, whatcha lookin' at?" She resumed her wild movements on the dance floor.

"Ol' Shawna really likes to party," said Josh. "She

sure is gettin' loose."

"Gettin' drunk is more like it," Melissa said. "I get so embarrassed for her. I'm sure glad I don't look like that!"

Me too, thought Serena.

Serena danced to several more numbers. Then the band stopped for a break and James came over to her.

"It's getting a little crazy around here. You want to leave? We could drive around for a while before I have to get you home."

"Good idea."

Later, James walked Serena to her door. "I've gotta play out of town tomorrow night," he said. "But I'll try to call you Sunday. Or you could call me."

Before she fell asleep that night, Serena reviewed the evening's events. It couldn't be better, she thought. The gymnastics meet, going out with James.... It was a night to remember.

Turn to page 53.

"Cat got your tongue, honey?" Serena's mom asked, turning to smile at her. "What time will you be home?"

"Umm, I guess about 3:00, Mom. I'll go tell Christy I can go."

* * *

At 11:55 Serena wheeled her bike into the shopping mall's huge parking lot. She locked it to the bike rack next to Christy's and looked around for her friend.

Christy was stationed on a large brick planter with a good view of the video arcade. "Nobody interesting yet," she reported as Serena approached. "Let's go find my shoes and get that part over with."

When they returned half an hour later, the video arcade was packed. Most of the kids were standing around one machine, cheering on the player.

"Mark, the Video King, is at it again," said a familiar voice.

"James! You scared me!"

"You don't look scared. In fact, you look great," he said.

"If it isn't the silver-tongued devil himself!" piped up Christy.

"Excuse my friend," said Serena, as she stepped warningly on Christy's toes. "She has this problem with her mouth."

"Not me, thanks." Christy said. *"I think beer is disgusting."*

"Would you and your friend like to go get a burger or something? I'm starving. Besides Mark'll probably be here all afternoon now that he's got an audience."

Time passed quickly as the friends ate, talked, and joked. Melissa Mendez and Shawna Rains joined them.

"Great party last night, huh, James?" said Melissa. "But you missed the fun part."

"Oh yeah? What was that?"

"When the cops came. Some of those dudes had a lot to drink. They were pretty wasted. Randall and Dale and some other guys started fighting. Dale got his face all cut up. And Randall almost got himself hauled off."

"Sounds like lots of fun," James replied. "I'm glad I left early."

"Well, we're gonna have a little party now over in the park if anyone's interested," chimed in Shawna. "Jason and Rick are gonna bring some six-packs."

"Not me, thanks." Christy got up. "I've gotta get home. Anyway, I think beer is disgusting. You coming, Serena?"

Reluctantly, Serena got up too. She didn't particularly want to go to the party. The idea of drinking beer in the park didn't appeal to her. First of all, she'd tried it once and didn't like the taste. Second, she didn't really know the other kids who were going to be there. And last, she didn't want to get busted! But she didn't want to leave James either.

She smiled as best she could. "I'll see you all later. Bye, James. It was nice seeing you."

"Hey, wait a minute!" James jumped up. "I'll walk you to your bike."

When they got to the bike rack, Christy quickly pedalled off. "I'll call you soon, Rena," she yelled.

Serena stood with James for a while. I could kick myself, she thought, for not staying longer. "I'm sorry," she began. "I'd like to come with you guys, but I told my mom...."

"Hey, it's all right. You gotta take care of business at home. Anyway, I'm not much into drinking. I mean...I don't know, it seems like such a waste. Besides I've got to rehearse some this afternoon and then we've got a gig tonight. I want to see you again though," he added, picking up her hand.

"That's okay with me," she said, smiling up into his eyes. Definitely one hundred percent okay, she thought.

THE END

"Cat got your tongue, honey?" Serena's mom asked, turning to smile at her. "What time will you be home?"

"Christy wants me to come over to her house after we go shopping. I'll be back by dinner time."

* * *

Serena arrived at the shopping mall a little before noon. She locked her bike to the bike rack and went to look for Christy. Since James and Mark hadn't shown up at the video arcade yet, the girls went off to shop for Christy's gym shoes.

James and Mark arrived a few minutes later by skateboard. "Well," Mark chuckled, rubbing his hands together, "time to go to work." Mark was the top scorer on most of the games in the arcade and was constantly trying to break his old records.

James wandered around the arcade. He played a couple of games, but his heart wasn't really in it. I wonder if she'll show, he thought.

By this time, Mark had drawn a small but noisy audience. James went over to check it out. He saw Serena and Christy at the edge of the crowd. They didn't notice him as he came up behind them.

"Mark, the Video King, is at it again," he said.

"James! You scared me!" exclaimed Serena.

Then the three of them decided to get hamburgers.

Time passed quickly as they ate, talked, and joked. Melissa Mendez and Shawna Rains joined them.

"Great party last night, huh, James?" said Melissa. "But you missed the fun part."

"Oh yeah? What was that?"

"When the cops came. Some of those dudes had a lot to drink. They were pretty wasted. Randall and Dale and some other guys started fighting. Dale got his face all cut up. And Randall almost got himself hauled off to jail."

"Sounds like lots of fun," James replied. "I'm glad I left early."

"Well, we're gonna have a little party now over in the park if anyone's interested," chimed in Shawna. "Jason and Rick are gonna bring some six-packs."

"Not me, thanks." Christy jumped up. "I've gotta get home. Anyway, I think beer is disgusting. You coming, Serena?"

"Uh, no. I can stick around for a while. I'll call you later, Christy." She turned back to the other kids.

"Let's go," said Shawna.

James hesitated. Hanging out in the park drinking beer wasn't really his idea of a good time. Besides he had a band rehearsal a little later on. If he drank, his coordination would be off and he wouldn't play as well. Still, he didn't want to leave Serena any sooner than he had to.

"You coming, James?" Melissa asked.

"Uh, sure. I can come for a little while," he replied.

The park was nearby, so Serena left her bike at the mall. James carried his skateboard. Melissa and Shawna had found a few more takers for their party. They were taking up a collection for more beer.

Serena and James lagged behind the others. They walked in silence. I really don't want to do this, James thought. It's such a waste. I should just tell Serena how I feel. But what if she gets mad? What if she thinks I'm boring? Or stuck-up? Or chicken? But she seems really level-headed so she'll probably understand. On the other hand, I guess I could just hang out for an hour or so....

What did James do?

Choice A
*If you think James told Serena he
didn't want to go drinking in the park,*
turn to page 39.

Choice B
*If you think James decided to go along
with the party,*
turn to page 42.

"Uh, listen, Serena," James began. "I have to tell you something."

Uh oh, she thought. He doesn't like me. He doesn't want to be with me. She stopped walking and looked at him. He seemed truly miserable. "What is it?" she asked softly.

"It's about this park thing. I'm not really into it. I mean, I just don't understand why some kids want to drink all the time. It seems like a waste of time to me. Besides I have a rehearsal in a little while."

Serena smiled. Then she started to laugh. "This is really silly," she said, between giggles. "I thought you wanted to go. I mean, these people are your friends, aren't they? I wanted to impress you, James! Anyway," she continued, "I'll tell you a secret. I hate beer!"

"Hey, Melissa! Shawna!" James called out. "We'll see you later. We have to go." He put his arm around Serena. "I'll walk you back to your bike."

They headed back, still chuckling. "That was a narrow escape," James declared, pretending to be serious.

"Thanks for rescuing me," Serena replied. They laughed all the way to the mall.

*   *   *

When Serena got home she went to the kitchen. Her mother was just putting down the phone.

"I just called Christy's," she said, "to ask you to pick up some milk on your way home. There wasn't any answer."

"Oh." Serena thought fast. "They had to go over to her grandma's. So I left. I can go back out if you want."

"No, that's okay. I'll drive. You want to come along?"

"Sure." Talk about narrow escapes! thought Serena.

"So did you have a good time, baby?" her mom asked.

"Yes...but I'm *not* a baby, in case you hadn't noticed."

"As a matter of fact, I have noticed. Your dad and I were just talking about how grown up you've become."

"Mom, I really wish you wouldn't call me 'baby' then. It's embarrassing."

"Well, I'll try. But you have to be patient with us old folks, ba—, I mean Serena. Old habits die hard, you know."

Serena and her mother laughed together. In the car, Serena talked about James.

"He certainly seems like a nice young man," her mom said. "I hope you'll be seeing more of him."

So do I, Serena thought. So do I.

THE END

"Uh, listen, Serena," James began. "I have to tell you something."

"What is it?"

Uh oh, James thought. It looks like she's upset already. Maybe I'll just go along with this party thing. I don't want to spoil her fun. "Oh...I don't...I can't...it's just that I can't stay too long. I have to rehearse some music this afternoon."

"That's okay," Serena responded. Secretly she felt relieved. She had thought he was going to say he didn't want to be with her or something like that. He looked so serious.

"Hey, you guys!" Melissa yelled. "You coming or not?"

They ran to catch up with the rest of the group.

When they got to the park, Jason and Rick were already there, along with a couple of guys who looked older. They were standing around a picnic table, drinking beer and smoking cigarettes. Music blared from a tape player.

Cans of beer were passed around from a large grocery bag. Serena sipped a little from her can. Yuck, she thought. Might as well get it over with. She drank several large swallows.

By the time she'd finished the can, she was thinking it didn't taste too bad. She was also enjoying the way she felt—relaxed, warm, carefree. She was usually shy around people she didn't know well, but now she talked and laughed easily.

She took another beer.

James was happy to be with Serena. But he was uneasy about her drinking. She was already starting a second beer!

He looked over at Rick and Jason who both played basketball for Rosemont. He hated seeing his teammates drinking like this. They sure are acting stupid, he thought.

But James knew he had to get to his rehearsal. He got up. "I'm outa here," he said. "See you later, Serena."

He set down the can of beer he'd been sipping. It was still almost full.

Wait! Serena wanted to say. Take me with you. She had come to the park to be with James and suddenly he was gone. "Bye," she said to his back as he hopped onto his skateboard.

As he skated toward home, James thought about the kids back at the park. Jason and Rick are really going to mess things up for the team if they don't straighten out, he thought. They've probably seen too many beer ads. The ones where all the team members are drinking and looking like they're having such a great time. Maybe Jason and Rick don't realize those guys are paid to look like they're having fun. They haven't figured

Serena had come to the park to be with James and suddenly he was gone. "Bye," she said to his back.

out that alcohol can wreck your body.

* * *

"So," said a deep voice, "now that he's gone maybe someone else can get a chance around here. My name's Duane. What's yours?" He put his arm around her.

"It's Serena."

Duane asked Serena lots of questions about herself and she found it easy to answer. She finished her second beer.

Duane was surprised to learn that she was fifteen. He said she acted much older. Melissa told him about Serena's skill as a gymnast.

"Let's see how you do it, Serena," Jason urged.

The others joined in. "Come on, Serena. Show us your moves."

Well, okay, why not? she thought. I'll just do a couple of floor exercises on the grass. She took off her jacket and walked to a smooth part of the lawn.

Feels kind of weird, she thought. The ground won't stay still. She ran forward a few steps and leaped into a somersault. She stumbled a little as she landed.

But her audience didn't seem to notice. They clapped for more. She bent over and kicked up into a handstand. She almost toppled over. Wow! she thought. The beer must really be affecting me.

"I've gotta go," she said.

Duane insisted on walking back to the mall with her. Actually she was glad he was there. Earlier she had felt relaxed and cheery, but now she felt wobbly and unsure of herself.

"You gonna be okay?" he asked as she fumbled with her bike lock.

"No problem," she said, hoping it was true.

She rode home slowly and cautiously. Serena Dawn Williams, she lectured, I hope you've learned something from this. You really could have hurt yourself today. You've got to take more control over your own life. Your health's more important than other peoples' opinions anyway!

When Serena arrived home, she found her parents sitting in the living room. They looked at her seriously.

"I called Christy's home several times this afternoon," her mother said. "There was no answer."

"You called Christy's? But why?" Serena was trying to think clearly. She knew she could be in big trouble.

"I wanted you to stop by the market for me. But that's not the point. The point is, where were you? We were starting to worry."

"I'm sorry. I guess we got back kind of late from shopping. Then we sat outside in the back yard and talked. I guess we just didn't hear the phone." She felt like crying.

Her mother came towards her. Oh please, thought Serena, don't let her smell my breath.

"What's the matter, baby?" her mom asked, putting her arms around her daughter. "It's okay. We're just a couple of old worry-warts, you know."

"It's okay, Mom," Serena mumbled. She pulled away and ran to her room. She lay down on her bed. Her head was beginning to ache.

Turn to page 53.

"How you doin'?" James asked. "I was getting...uh...I was getting a little concerned about you." He led her away from the group.

"Oh," Serena said. "Why's that?"

"Well," he started. Here goes nothin', he thought. "I didn't know if you were used to drinking. I thought maybe you should slow down."

"I see."

"Serena, I'm not putting you down or anything. I just thought...."

She interrupted, "You thought what? Serena's too young to drink? Too much of a baby to handle it? If you thought that, why'd you even ask me here?" She pulled away and ran down the steps.

I've blown it totally, James thought. He wondered what he should do next. Go after her? Wait for her to cool off and then look for her? Go back to his music and forget the whole thing? He slammed his fist against the porch railing.

"Where's your friend, James? You scare her away?" It was Randall. "Maybe I should see if I can find her."

"Forget it, man," James answered, starting down the steps toward the parked cars.

He found her leaning against his car. She was crying. "Serena, I'm so sorry...."

"Oh James!" She paused and sniffed. "I'm the one who's sorry. I don't know what's wrong with me."

He put his arm around her. "Listen," he said. "The thing is...well...my old man used to have a drinking problem. I mean a really bad drinking problem. Maybe I worry too much about it, but I've seen the damage drinking can do. I guess I just got carried away."

"I'm glad you were worried about me. I mean, I never drink, so I don't know what to expect. But I really don't want to make a fool of myself, and I'm afraid that's just what I did!" She sniffed again.

James unlocked the car and reached inside. He handed her a tissue. "How about us two fools gettin' out of here? We still have time to go for a drive before you have to be home."

"I'd like that a lot." She smiled.

Later, James walked Serena to her door. "I've gotta play out of town tomorrow night," he said. "But I'll call you Sunday. Or you can call me."

Before she fell asleep that night, Serena reviewed the evening's events. The gymnastics meet had been thrilling. And being with James was wonderful. He really must like me, Serena thought. He cares enough to be honest with me. She sighed and smiled. It was a night to remember.

THE END

"Well," James said, smiling and slipping his arm around Serena, "It looks like you're having a good time."

"It's a fun party," she said. "The music's great too. How come you stopped playing?"

"I...uh...I just wanted to get some fresh air, you know. It gets stuffy in there. The smoke gets to me too."

"Are you going to play some more?"

"You trying to get rid of me?"

"Are you crazy?" she laughed. "I really like to hear you play."

"Yeah, I'll play some more," he said. "I need to get something to drink first."

Someone handed him a beer. He sipped a little of it and then set the can down. "I guess I'll go back in. What about you?"

"I'll be there in a minute," said Serena. She picked up the can he'd been drinking from and took a sip.

"You take care now," he said seriously.

"Don't worry about me, James!" She gave him a playful push and took another sip. She really didn't mind the taste at all now. She was getting a strange, floaty feeling.

The rest of the evening passed in a blur of sound and movement. She was starting on her fourth beer when James took her by the arm. "Time to be getting you home," he said.

As they went down the porch steps, Serena lost her footing. James caught her as she pitched forward.

"I guess I'm not as coordinated as I was earlier," she said with an uncertain laugh. The coach would die if he knew, she thought. So would my parents. So will I if they see me like this! These were sobering thoughts.

"You okay?" asked James as he helped her into the car.

"I don't know. I was just thinking...maybe I shouldn't go home yet.... Maybe I should get some coffee...."

James started the engine and eased the car out onto the street. I should've tried to stop her from drinking so much, he thought. At least I could have said something. He sighed. "Well, if you've had too much to drink, coffee won't help. What you need is time and we don't have much of that. I hate to think what your old man will do to me if you're not home at 11:00."

"I hate to think what he'll do to me if he sees me like this," she moaned. She was feeling sick to her stomach.

"You need to throw up?"

"I don't think so. I just want to go home and go to bed."

They drove the rest of the way in silence.

When they pulled up in front of Serena's house, James handed her some breath mints. "Just in case you run into your parents. They might help." He helped her out of the car.

"Thanks. I'm sorry, James. I really had a good time. I feel like I've ruined everything." She was chewing up the mints as fast as she could.

"Don't worry about it. It's okay. You just take care of yourself."

Serena let herself in the door quietly. She tiptoed down the hall toward her room.

"That you, baby?" came her father's voice from her parents' bedroom. "How was your evening?"

"Yes, it's me, Daddy." And I'm not a baby, she thought. "I'll tell you all about it in the morning," she called through the door. "I'm really tired."

"All right, sweetheart. Good night."

"'Night, Daddy."

Thank goodness, thought Serena, as she crawled beneath the covers of her bed. Safe at last! Girl, you are a fool, she thought. Then she fell asleep.

Serena slept late Saturday morning. When she finally woke up, she had a splitting headache. Her memories of the previous night's party were hazy. She couldn't remember much about how she'd gotten home. She moaned softly into her pillow. I hope I didn't make a total fool of myself, she thought.

Turn to page 53.

Continued from page 30, 47 or 52

On Monday Serena didn't see James until their fifth period geometry class. He slipped into the seat behind her.

"I tried to call you last night," he whispered.

She turned around. "I was out with my folks. They had some concert tickets and I couldn't think of a way to get out of it."

"What group did you see?"

"Not a group, silly. It was classical music."

"Well, it must have been *some* kind of group...."

"Serena. James. Would one of you like to demonstrate your proof for problem 4?"

"Uh, no thanks, Mr. Davis," answered James quickly.

Some students in the class snickered, and Mr. Davis wrote something in his notebook.

Serena didn't dare turn around again.

After class she walked with James to his locker. "I have to see Coach Walters about basketball after school," he said. "But I'll call you tonight if you promise to be home."

"Definitely," she said. "I've got to study for my geography midterm."

* * *

Sixth period art class went quickly. Serena spent the hour chatting with Tracy while they worked on their papier maché animals.

The final bell rang and they headed for their lockers. They were getting their books out when Melissa and Shawna walked by.

"Hi, Serena. How you doin'? Hi, Tracy," Shawna said, coming over to them.

Serena and Tracy greeted her and Melissa.

"You want to come with us over to Josh's?" Melissa asked. "They have a pool table and Josh promised to make strawberry margaritas."

"Oh, well...I don't know," began Serena.

"Not me," said Tracy. "I have to practice for drama club."

Shawna and Melissa looked at Serena, waiting for her answer. "C'mon," urged Shawna. "It'll be so cool."

Serena didn't want to disappoint her friends. But she wasn't sure she wanted to drink margaritas—even with strawberries. She thought about what her parents would do if they found out.

"C'mon, Rena," urged Melissa. "It'll be fun."

Well, Serena thought. I could go and just not drink much of anything. But my folks....

What did Serena do?

Choice A
If you think Serena decided not *to go to Josh's,*
turn to page 56.

Choice B
If you think Serena decided to go to Josh's,
turn to page 59.

Besides, Serena thought, I really should go work out this afternoon to be in shape for tomorrow's practice. Plus there's my midterm.

"Sorry," she said to Melissa and Shawna. "I've got plans. But thanks for asking me." I hope they'll still like me, she thought.

"Aw, come on, Serena," said Shawna.

"No, I really can't."

Serena and Tracy got their books from the locker and Tracy left for drama practice.

Serena was walking home when she heard the rumble of skateboard wheels behind her.

"Hey, beautiful!"

"Hi, James. I thought you were going to see the coach."

"Yeah. I went over to the gym but he's in some meeting. I guess I'll have to see him tomorrow."

"Mmm," she nodded. She smiled at him as he walked beside her, carrying his skateboard.

"So where are you going? Home?" he asked.

"Uh huh. Then I'm gonna go work out. Then for fun I'm going to study geography."

He gave her a curious look. "For fun?"

"That's a joke, James. Ha ha, you know. Even I don't think geography's fun."

"You know...I really respect the way you have your life together," James said. "Like...I just ran into Shawna and Melissa. They're gonna go party somewhere. I mean, I like to party too...but there's gotta be somethin' else."

"Yeah, I guess so. But sometimes I feel like I'm missing out on a lot of fun."

They walked in silence for a while.

"Well, I'll tell you one thing," James said as they neared Serena's house. "I think you're going to have a good influence on me."

Serena laughed. She shook her head. "I'm not *that* good! Anyway—I think you're a good influence on me. 'Cause, well...I think you're really understanding."

"Thanks," he said. "That's really nice of you to say."

"I guess I'd better go in."

"Yeah." He took her hand and squeezed it. "I'll call you for sure."

"Okay. Bye. Take care," she said.

I sure am lucky, she thought as she ran up the walk to her door.

James hopped on his skateboard and started off. I sure am lucky, he thought.

THE END

"I think you're going to have a good influence on me,"
James said.

"Sure," Serena said, "but I can only stay a little while."

"Well, come on then," said Shawna, taking her by the arm.

As Serena, Shawna, and Melissa headed up the street they met James on his skateboard. He slowed down as he passed them.

"Hey, you want to come party with us?" Shawna called. "We're goin' over to Josh's."

He shook his head. He gave Serena a puzzled look. "Are you going over there?"

"Yes, I'm going over there. Is something wrong with that?" She was surprised at how angry she sounded. But, she thought, it really isn't any of his business.

"Hey, lighten up. I'm just kind of surprised. See you later, okay?" He skated off.

Serena was left with a sinking feeling. She wondered if she was making a mistake.

*   *   *

Later on at Josh's house, she forgot her concerns. About six other kids had showed up. Josh had made several batches of strawberry margaritas in the blender. The stereo was going full blast.

Serena felt lightheaded. Worries about school, about her parents, about James were a million miles away.

Passing tests, winning meets, and getting approval weren't important to her now. It was such a relief to not have to think about those things....

Shawna and a guy named Brian were dancing on the pool table. Serena thought it was one of the funniest things she'd ever seen.

"Hey! You guys!" It was Josh yelling. He went over to the stereo and shut it off. "You're going to wreck the table. Come on, get off."

Brian and Shawna got down. The party mood was broken.

"I guess we'd better start cleaning up," someone said.

"What time is it?" someone else asked.

Serena looked at her watch. Almost 6:00! Already! Oh no, she thought. She generally didn't have to be home until 5:00 on school days. But she hadn't even told her mom where she was going this afternoon. And it would be after 6:00 by the time she walked home. What am I going to do? she wondered.

She gathered up some glasses. This place sure is messed up, she thought. Josh's folks are going to flip out.

Josh didn't seem too concerned though. "So how'd you like my party?" he asked when she brought the glasses into the kitchen.

Serena set the glasses down and leaned unsteadily against the counter. "It was real fun. But I don't feel so hot now. And I've gotta get home fast!"

"You need a ride?" It was Brian. "I'm gonna take Shawna home, and probably Kelly and Jason, too."

"Oh, thanks!" Serena said. Then she paused and tried to think clearly. Her folks always made such a big deal about drinking and driving. And, deep down, she knew they were right. The news was full of stories about horrible accidents caused by drunk drivers.

Well, maybe Brian's not drunk, she thought. He seems okay now. Maybe he's just a little high. Besides, this is an emergency....

What did Serena do?

Choice A
If you think Serena decided it was all right to accept the ride,
turn to page 66.

Choice B
If you think Serena decided not *to accept the ride,*
turn to page 62.

Well, Serena thought, I guess I'd rather take my chances with my parents than with a driver who's been drinking.

"You ready?" Brian asked.

"Oh, uh...on second thought, I guess I'd better walk."

"What's the matter, Serena? You afraid to drive with me? You think I'm drunk or something?" he demanded.

"It's just that I need the exercise...for my gymnastics...you know."

"Suit yourself," said Brian. "We're outa here."

Serena debated whether or not to call her parents. She took a deep breath and began dialing.

"Mom? Hi, it's me....I'm okay....I'm over at Josh's, but I'm leaving for home right now, okay?...It won't be dark yet. I'll hurry....No really, I want to walk. See you in a few minutes."

Well, at least that went all right, Serena thought. She found her school books and said goodbye to Josh and the kids who still remained. She zipped up her jacket and started home.

As an experiment she tried walking in a straight line along the sidewalk's edge. She could only go four or five steps without veering to one side or the other. It seemed kind of funny to her, but the thought of her parents kept her from laughing.

She was tired when she reached her house. She entered the front door as quietly as she could and ran for the bathroom. She locked the door. She washed her hands and face. She brushed her teeth. She gargled mouthwash. She leaned her head against the cool tile wall.

"Serena, is that you?"

"Yes, Daddy."

"I didn't hear you come in. Are you all right?"

Serena came out of the bathroom. "Dad, I feel kind of sick. Maybe I'm getting the flu or something. I'm gonna go lie down, okay?"

Mr. Williams went into the kitchen. "Denise," he said, "Serena says she isn't feeling well. But I wonder if she didn't have something to drink over at the Kellers. Dave and Marjorie are at a conference tonight, you know. And Serena came out of the bathroom smelling like mouthwash and who knows what else."

"Oh, Donald, surely Serena has more sense than that." She looked at her husband hopefully.

"Go take a look for yourself," he said.

Serena's mother put a cool hand on her daughter's forehead. "So what's the matter, sugar?" she asked softly.

"Oh, Mom, I feel awful," Serena moaned. It was true too. "I just want to go to sleep."

Serena's mom kissed her and quietly closed the door.

"I believe you're right," she said to her husband when

she came back into the kitchen. "But I think we can deal with it later. She seems to be miserable enough at the moment."

She paused and then sighed. "I just don't understand it. Serena, of all people! This just isn't like her."

* * *

Serena wasn't at school the next day. James looked for her during lunch. He spotted Tracy and Christy and asked them if they'd seen her.

"She wasn't in English," said Christy. "She must be sick."

James went to a telephone. "How *are* you?" he began when he heard her voice. "I was getting worried."

"Well, that's kind of hard to say. I feel awful. I have a horrible headache. And I'm grounded for a month. On the other hand, I'm not in juvenile hall like Shawna. Did you hear what happened?"

"I heard Brian got busted for drunk driving with a bunch of kids in his car. I was afraid you were with them," said James.

"I almost was."

"When I called you last night, your dad just said you weren't available. He sounded kind of mad."

"I guess he thought maybe you were involved. Brian's dad called him this morning 'cause they need a lawyer for Brian," said Serena.

"So how come Shawna's in juvey?" James asked.

"She sassed the police officer or something. Anyway they took her away and her mom wouldn't come get her."

"Oh, Serena, how did you get yourself in such a mess?"

"I don't know, James. I don't even like drinking! And I *hate* the way I feel now! I wouldn't blame you if you never spoke to me again. I feel like such a fool!"

"Now *that's* foolish! But what does 'grounded' mean? Can we see each other?"

"Just at school, I guess. And I can only talk on the phone for five minutes at a time. In fact, my mom just came in. I have to get off now."

"Okay, but I'll see you at school tomorrow, right?"

"Oh for sure, James. I'm so glad you called."

She put down the phone and walked carefully to the bathroom. She took two aspirins and drank two glasses of water. Then she stared at herself in the mirror. "You look awful," she said. "I hope you've learned something from all this."

THE END

"You ready to go now?" Brian asked.

"I just have to find my books," Serena answered.

Five minutes later Brian was driving Serena and the other kids home.

Shawna was turning the radio dial, trying to find a station she liked.

"Leave the dial alone, Shawna," Brian said, pushing at her hand.

"C'mon, jus' let me find somethin', " she insisted.

"I said cut it out!" Brian grabbed for Shawna's hand

At the police station, Serena sat in a small room with Kelly, Jason and Jeff.

and the car swerved.

Maybe I'd better get out and walk, Serena thought. She had just worked up the courage to ask Brian to stop and let her out when he began to swear. Then she heard the siren.

* * *

Later, at the police station, Serena sat in a small room with Kelly, Jason, and Jeff. Through a window to the next room they could see Brian as the police took his fingerprints. He'd been arrested for driving under the influence of alcohol.

I wish I could just disappear, she thought.

They didn't know where Shawna was. When the policewoman had told Shawna to get into the patrol car, she had refused. The officer called for assistance and another patrol car arrived. Shawna, crying and fighting, had been handcuffed and put into the other car.

Serena and the others were waiting for their parents. They didn't talk much. Kelly was crying softly. I wish I could just disappear, Serena thought. I can't believe myself!

The police officer who had stopped them came in. "You know," she said, "you kids are lucky. You could all be dead. Did you know that 8,000 teenagers are killed in drunk-driving accidents every year? That's about 22 deaths every day! And something like 40,000 kids are injured every year. Permanently. You could all be statistics." She sighed and shook her head. "Jeff, your parents are here. And yours too, Serena. Come with me."

When Serena saw her parents, she burst into tears. Her mother put her arms around her. But her father didn't touch her. He barely even looked at her. "I'm so disappointed in you, young lady. I don't even know what to say."

That night Serena cried herself to sleep.

*   *   *

The next morning she felt awful. Her head felt like it would split open. She felt dizzy and sick to her stomach.

Then her parents came into her room to talk to her and she felt even worse. Her father was still very cool to her and her mother was fighting back the tears.

"How could you do this to us?" her father asked.

"Daddy, I didn't do it to you! Can't you see I did it to myself? Can't I even make my own mistakes?"

"You've done it to yourself, all right," he said. "Your mother and I have decided to ground you until the end of the school year."

"Oh, Daddy, no! You can't mean that! It's not fair!" She was angry now.

Her mother was crying. "We're sorry, Serena. But we feel it will help you in the long run."

Serena threw herself onto her bed and sobbed. Her parents left the room. It's not fair, she told herself over and over.

Later on her mother came in to ask her if she wanted something to eat. "I'm not hungry," Serena said. She gave her mother a hurt look.

"Your father's going into his office now. Brian Mac-Donald's parents called him. They need a lawyer for Brian."

"Oh great," said Serena. "Daddy'll probably get Brian locked up for life."

Serena's mother went out, closing the door behind her.

Around noon, the phone rang. Serena picked up the receiver of her bedside extension.

"Hello?"

"How *are* you?" It was James. "I was getting worried!"

"Oh James, I can't believe this mess. Did you hear what happened?"

"I heard that Brian MacDonald got busted for drunk driving and some other kids were with him. Were *you* there?"

"It was horrible." She started to cry again. "They took Shawna away to juvenile hall. And I'm grounded till the end of the school year! All I was doing was riding in the car!"

"Oh, babe, I'm so sorry." James was silent for a long moment. Then he said, "But that's not exactly all you were doing."

"What do you mean?"

"Well, you did get into the car, right? How come you did that, Serena? You must not have been thinking so clearly yourself."

"Are you saying I was drunk?"

"Listen, Serena, please just listen before you get all

bent out of shape. I'm worried about you, okay? Drinking can be a dangerous thing. I know what I'm talking about. Remember I told you about my dad? Before he stopped drinking? He hit a little girl on a bike, Serena. She almost died. He wouldn't even admit there was a problem till that happened."

"James, I really don't think I have that kind of problem." Serena was hoping for sympathy from him and all she was getting was another lecture. "Anyway, I have to hang up. My mom's here."

"Okay. But will you think about what I'm saying, please. And one more thing. I was thinking maybe you'd like to talk to my sister—you know, Charlene—the one that's a junior? Anyway, she used to have some problems with drinking and she knows a lot about it. I know she'd be happy to talk to you. Think about it, okay?"

"Okay, James." She sighed.

"I really care about you," he said. Then he hung up.

"James wants me to talk to his sister about drinking." she told her mother. "It's not like I had a problem."

Or do I? she thought. Sometimes I feel like two people. One wants to be Miss Perfect and the other just wants to get away from it all.

But still, she thought, it's my own business. I can still drink if I want to. I just have to be more careful.

It's my life and I should be able to do what I want.

Serena's mother spoke. "That might be a good idea, baby."

I'm not a baby, Serena thought. And I don't need to talk to anybody, either.

But all afternoon she kept thinking of James' words, "I really care about you."

What did Serena do?

Choice A
If you think Serena decided she could manage on her own,
turn to page 73.

Choice B
If you think Serena decided to talk to Charlene,
turn to page 77.

In the weeks that followed the incident with the police, Serena saw James every day in geometry class. Sometimes he came over to her house after school. But it seemed like they always ended up arguing.

James thought Serena was drinking too much. "You think *anything's* too much," she told him. "You sound like my parents. Besides I barely get the chance to drink now that I'm grounded."

James tried to explain why he was worried about her. He thought that she was using alcohol as a way to avoid facing her problems.

"It's true," she said. "When I've had a drink it makes me more relaxed. Then I don't worry so much about being Miss Perfect. I can just be myself. What's wrong with that?"

"Oh, Serena," James sighed. "Nothing's wrong with being yourself. That's just the problem—I miss the 'old' you. I want my Serena back!"

* * *

James finally decided he had to do something to change his life. He was worrying about Serena too much. And he wasn't really enjoying their time together anymore.

He wrote her a letter. "We have to face the fact that there's no future for us," he wrote. "Things just aren't

Serena sat on her bed with James' letter in her hand.
I wish I knew what to do, she thought.

like they used to be. I still care about you, but I have to let you go. Love, James." He walked to a corner mailbox and dropped in the letter. On the way back home, he couldn't help crying.

Serena sat on her bed with James' letter in her hand. She was crying. I wish I knew what to do, she thought. Maybe I should call Charlene.

Then she felt a flash of anger at James. It's none of his business if I want to drink sometimes, she told herself. Anyway, there are lots of other guys out there. I just need to get out and meet some of them!

What did Serena do?

Choice A
If you think Serena decided to forget about James,
turn to page 76.

Choice B
If you think Serena decided to call Charlene for help,
turn to page 77.

Serena did her best to put James out of her mind. She spent time with Melissa and Shawna. A few times, she sneaked out of the house to see guys. She tried to keep busy, but she often found herself bursting into tears.

She missed some practice sessions for gymnastics. Her coach told her he was worried.

Serena was worried too, but she didn't feel she could explain it to anyone. Sometimes she would take James' letter out of the drawer where she kept it. Reading it always made her cry. "He just doesn't understand," she thought. "Nobody understands."

THE END

Serena and Tracy met at their locker after last period. "You look so great these days, Rena!" Tracy commented. "I was getting worried for a while there," she added in a lower voice. "You seemed so down."

Serena gave her friend's arm an affectionate squeeze. "Thanks, Trace. I know. I'm sorry I kind of flaked out on everybody. I'm so glad you're still my friend."

"Do you think you can come over later?" Tracy wanted to know.

"Well, I'm supposed to meet Charlene in a few minutes. But I can come over after I see her. You can wait with me if you want."

"Okay. She sure seems nice. It's hard to believe she had all those problems with drinking and drugs that James told us about."

"Yeah, I know. But she really did. She even had to go to the hospital because she mixed drugs and alcohol. They thought she was going to have permanent brain damage. Can you believe that? Now she's junior class president!"

"It blows my mind," said Tracy. "The things some people do. Look, here comes Charlene!"

The three girls walked slowly down the school steps and along the sidewalk. They were enjoying each other's company. Serena was telling Tracy how much Charlene had helped her.

"Don't believe everything you hear," Charlene said

with a smile. "This girl was ready to help herself. She just needed a couple of suggestions."

"No, really," said Serena. "Seriously! I was so scared and I felt so alone. I almost didn't even call you."

"Well, I must admit I am pretty frightening," said Charlene.

"You know that's not what I mean! Admitting that I needed help was one of the hardest things I've ever done. Everything since then has been almost easy!"

"Easy, huh? I thought you worked pretty hard. It wasn't so easy for you to talk about what was bothering you at first. And it took a lot of courage for you to start letting your parents know how you were really feeling."

"Well, maybe it was hard at first. But then I found out I actually *like* to talk about my feelings."

"Now you can't shut her up," laughed Charlene. Then she turned to Serena. "You've got a lot to be proud of, you know. You've come a long way."

* * *

Serena and James were sitting on the school steps during lunch.

"You happy, Rena?"

"Mmm," she nodded. "You can tell, can't you?" She leaned against him and closed her eyes, enjoying the

"I feel so lucky," Serena said to James. *"I feel like I got my life back."*

feeling of the sun on her skin. "I feel so lucky. I feel like I got my life back. And I love Charlene so much!"

"She's okay, for a sister."

"Very funny. Anyway, I was just thinking if it weren't for you and Charlene, I probably never would've gotten off being grounded. I still can't believe you talked my dad into it."

"I didn't exactly talk him into it. He was really impressed by your change in attitude. He really loves you. He just had trouble accepting that you're not perfect."

"I know, I know. But you guys convinced me that there were other ways to solve my problems besides drinking. Like *communicating,* for instance."

"I guess I am pretty wonderful, huh?" James poked Serena in the ribs and she jumped.

"Cut it out. We've got to get to class. You know what else is great?" she asked as they walked back into the school.

"No, what?"

"They don't call me 'baby' anymore."

THE END

About this Book

Serena's Secret is part of an important new series of books designed
to help young people make informed, responsible decisions about
drug use. Other books in the series include *Danny's Dilemma* and
Christy's Chance. They combine substance abuse information and
models for resisting peer pressure in the popular interactive adven-
ture book format.

The development of these books was supported by funds from
the National Institute of Child Health and Development. They have
gone through extensive pretesting with preadolescents and have
been carefully reviewed by substance abuse professionals. The com-
mittee of professionals not only gave initial input to determine ap-
propriate content, but also reviewed the books during their
development.

About the Authors

Christine DeVault and Bryan Strong, PhD, are educators who have
authored numerous elementary, middle school and college texts
in sociology, psychology and family life.

Also available as part of this series are three companion nonfiction
books, *Alcohol: The Real Story, Tobacco: The Real Story,* and *Marijuana: The Real Story.* Each book provides up-to-date facts and information about the use and abuse of alcohol, tobacco and
marijuana. They are compact, easy to read and reinforced with il-
lustrations and challenging case study scenarios.